Mr. Ott Is a Crackpot!

Dan Gutman

Pictures by
Jim Paillot

HARPER
An Imprint of HarperCollinsPublishers

To Jay Barton

My Weirder-est School #10: Mr. Ott Is a Crackpot!
Text copyright © 2022 by Dan Gutman
Illustrations copyright © 2022 by Jim Paillot
All rights reserved. Printed in the United States of America.

Library of Congress Control Number: 2021948096
ISBN 978-0-06-291082-0 (pbk bdg) — ISBN 978-0-06-291083-7 (trade bdg)

Typography by Martha Maynard
22 23 24 25 26   PC/BRR   10 9 8 7 6 5 4 3 2 1
❖
First Edition

Contents

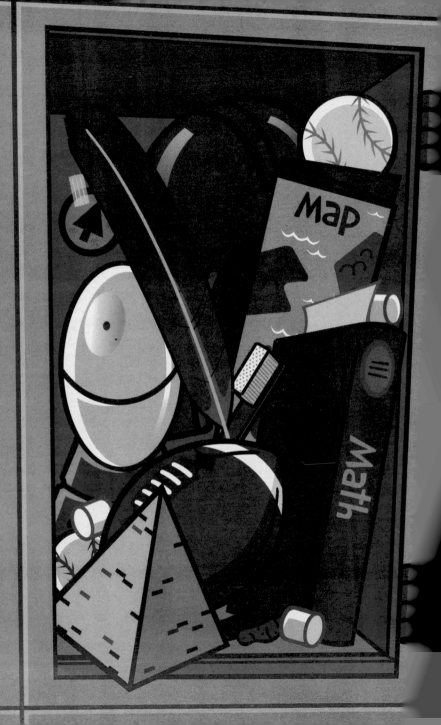

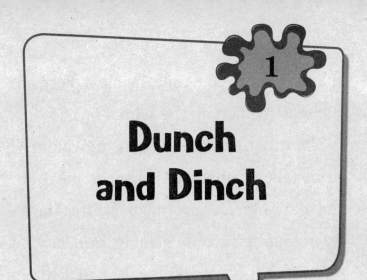

Dunch and Dinch

My name is A.J. and I know what you're thinking. You're thinking about eating. I know, because that's what I'm thinking about.

My friend Ryan thinks about eating all the time. He'll eat *anything*, even stuff that isn't food. One time, he ate a piece of the seat cushion on the school bus.*

The other day, we were in the vomitorium talking about our favorite meal of the day. My favorite meal is breakfast. Ryan said his favorite meal is brunch.

"Brunch isn't a real meal," I told him. "It's just breakfast and lunch at the same time."

"In my family, we call that lunfast," said Michael, who never ties his shoes. "It's lunch and breakfast together."

"Your family is weird," I told Michael.

"*Our* family likes to combine lunch and dinner," said Alexia, this girl who rides a

---

*He put ketchup on it first.

2

skateboard all the time. "We call it linner."

"That's not linner," said Neil, who we call the nude kid even though he wears clothes. "In my family, lunch and dinner together is lupper."

"That's lunner," said Michael.

"Do you know what *my* family calls lunch and dinner?" asked Ryan. "Dunch."

"We call lunch and dinner dinch," said Michael.

"What?!" I said. "Dunch and dinch aren't words."

"They are too."

"Are not."

Dunch and dinch are definitely not words. You should look them up in a dictionary. I bet they're not there.

"Sometimes, *my* family has breakfast for dinner," said Andrea, this annoying girl with curly brown hair. "We call it brinner."

"I agree with Andrea," said her crybaby friend Emily, who always agrees with Andrea.

Breakfast for dinner? What's up with *that*? I could see eating breakfast for lunch, or lunch for breakfast. I could see eating lunch for dinner, or dinner for lunch. But eating breakfast for dinner? If you ask me, that should be illegal. Meals should stay in their own lane.

Food is weird.

Bok! Bok! Bok!

You probably think this book will be about food. Well, you're wrong! It has *nothing* to do with food. Why do books have to start out with stuff that relates to the rest of the book? Who made up *that* dumb rule?

Anyway, after dunch—I mean lunch—we went back to class with Mr. Cooper.

"Turn to page twenty-three in your math books," he told us.

Ugh. I hate math.

That's when the weirdest thing in the history of the world happened. An announcement came over the loudspeaker.

Well, that's not the weird part. Announcements come over the loudspeaker all the time. The weird part was what happened next.

"Mr. Cooper, please turn on your smartboard," announced Mrs. Patty, our school secretary.

Mr. Cooper turned on the smartboard. And you'll never believe in a million hundred years whose face appeared on the screen.

It was Morgan Brocklebank!

"BOOOOOOOOO!" Everybody started booing.

Morgan Brocklebank is this mean girl

who goes to Dirk School on the other side of town. We call it "Dork School." Morgan does the Dirk morning announcements every day.

"Well, hello, Ella Mentry School *losers*!" said Morgan.

Morgan has hated us ever since her methane-powered car, "The Dirkmobile," exploded and we won the Brain Games. The whole place smelled like cow farts. (You can read about it in a book called *Miss Brown Is Upside Down!*)

"What can we do for you, Miss Brocklebank?" asked Mr. Cooper.

"I have a challenge for you," Morgan replied.

"We accept!" I shouted.

Mr. Cooper held up his hand and shushed me.

"Hold on, A.J.," he said. "You don't even know what she's challenging us to do yet."

"Our class challenges your class to a softball game," said Morgan, "to raise money for charity."

"Softball?" whispered Alexia. "I've never played softball."

"Me neither," whispered Neil.

"I take pitching lessons after school," bragged Andrea.

Ugh. Andrea takes lessons in *everything* after school. If they gave lessons in cleaning out your earwax, she would take those lessons so she could get better at it. What is her problem?

"Which charity are you raising money for?" asked Mr. Cooper.

"We're fighting a serious disease," replied Morgan Brocklebank. "Freckles."

WHAT?

"Since when are freckles a disease?" asked Ryan.

"I have freckles," said Andrea.

"Me too," said Emily, who has everything Andrea has.

"Me three," said Michael.

"Oh no!" shouted Ryan. "We're all gonna die . . . from freckles!"

"Run for your lives!" shouted Neil.

"We've got to *do* something!" said Emily, and then she went running out of the room.

That's ridorkulous. Lots of people have freckles. There's nothing wrong with freckles.

"That's a dumb charity," Neil shouted at the smartboard. "Go find another class to challenge."

Up on the screen, Morgan sneered.

"Oh, I guess you're *afraid* to play us," she said. "I guess you're a bunch of scaredy-cats and chickens. *Bok! Bok! Bok!*"*

Morgan Brocklebank does a terrible

---

*It could also be spelled "buck," "balk," or "bock." But we decided to go with "bok."

chicken imitation.

"Hey, nobody calls *us* chickens!" said Michael.

"That's right," I said. "We're not gonna take that! We have to play them."

"Let's beat those Dirk dorks!" shouted Ryan.

"Yeah!"

"Yeah!"

"Yeah!"

In case you were wondering, everybody was shouting "Yeah!"

"Well, it looks like my class accepts your challenge," said Mr. Cooper.

"Good," said Morgan. "Next Saturday. In the field behind our school. Be there or be square. And I still say you're chickens. *Bok! Bok! Bok!*"

3

Duck

Mr. Cooper turned off the smartboard.

"Okay, open your math books," he said. "Any questions about page twenty-three?"

"Yeah," I said. "Will you coach our class in the softball game against Dirk School?"

"Uh, no," Mr. Cooper replied. "I don't know anything about coaching softball."

Bummer in the summer!

"Maybe Miss Small will coach us," said Ryan.

Miss Small is our fizz ed teacher. She's really good at sports.

"Miss Small broke her leg falling out of a tree over the weekend," said Andrea.

Not *again*! Miss Small is *always* falling out of trees. (You can read about it in a book called *Miss Small Is off the Wall!*)

What were we going to do? We needed a coach if we were going to beat Dirk School.*

And you'll never believe who walked into the door at that moment.

---

*Hey, when is Mr. Ott going to show up?

15

Nobody! Who walks into doors? That would hurt. But you'll never believe who walked into the door*way*.

It was our principal, Mr. Klutz! He has no hair at all. I mean *none*. He looks a little bit like Mr. Clean.

"I just heard about your softball game against Dirk School," Mr. Klutz said. "How exciting!"

"We need a coach," said Alexia. "Will you coach us, Mr. Klutz? The game is next Saturday."

"Uh, sorry," said Mr. Klutz. "This is a busy week for me."

"Please, please, please?" we begged.

We put on our best puppy dog faces. That's when you make your face look like a cute little puppy dog's. It usually works. Grown-ups will do anything if you put on a puppy dog face.

"After school on Tuesday, I have to *blah blah blah blah*," said Mr. Klutz. "On

Wednesday after school, I have to *blah blah blah blah . . ."*

He went on like that for a million hundred seconds.

"Where are we gonna get a coach?" asked Neil.

"Hmmmm," Mr. Klutz said as he rubbed his chin.

Grown-ups always say "Hmmmm" and rub their chin when they don't have any ideas. Nobody knows why.

"I've got it!" Mr. Klutz finally said, snapping his fingers.

Grown-ups always snap their fingers when they get a good idea. Nobody knows why.

"There's a man named Willie Ott who lives in town," Mr. Klutz told us. "He used to be a big league coach. I bet he would help you."

"Will you ask him?" Andrea said.

"No, but *you* can ask him," said Mr. Klutz. "Let's go to his house!"

Mr. Klutz walked out of the room and we all rushed to follow him. Yay! No math! We were going on a field trip to Willie Ott's house.

Field trips are cool. Well, except for field trips to a field. Those field trips are boring.

We left Ella Mentry School and made a left at the corner. Then we made a right at the next corner. Then we made another left at the corner after that.

But who cares? Don't you hate it when they give directions in books? You're not going to that place. So why would you care about how to get there?

Finally, we reached the street where Willie Ott lives.

"There's Mr. Ott's house," Mr. Klutz said as he pointed. "They used to call him Duck."

"Why, does he look like a duck?" I asked.

"I don't know why," said Mr. Klutz. "Whatever you do, don't call him Duck. I heard it makes him mad."

We climbed the stairs to Willie Ott's house. An old man on the front porch was sitting in a rocking chair.

"Mr. Ott," said Mr. Klutz. "I'm the principal at Ella Mentry School. And these are some of my third graders."

"Pleased to meet you," said Willie Ott, waving to us.

"We heard you used to be a ballplayer," said Andrea.

"Oh, that was a *long* time ago," Willie Ott replied. "I was a young man then."

"Did you play in the big leagues?" asked Michael.

Willie Ott sighed and closed his eyes for a moment.

"Yup," he said. "For a day. I had one major league game at bat."

"Just *one*?" Neil asked.

"Yup, it was during the World Series," said Willie Ott.

"What happened?" asked Andrea.

"It was the bottom of the ninth inning," Willie explained.

"Yeah?"

"The score was tied."

"Yeah?"

"Two outs."

"Yeah?"

"Full count."

"Yeah?"

"There was a runner on second base."

"Yeah?"

"If I got a hit, we'd win the World Series."

"Yeah?"

"It was all up to me. All my life had led up to that moment."

"So what happened?" asked Alexia.

"I got hit in the head by the ball," Willie told us.

"What happened after that?" I asked.

"I don't know," he replied. "I was unconscious. I didn't wear a batting helmet back then. All I know is, we lost the game and the World Series. I never played again."

There was a sad look on Willie Ott's face. I guess he never got over what happened.

"Why did they call you Duck?" I asked him.

"Arlo!" whispered Andrea. "Mr. Klutz told us not to call him Duck!"

"I didn't call him Duck!" I explained. "I just asked why they called him Duck."

It looked like Mr. Ott might start crying. A tear slid down his cheek.

"They called me Duck," he said quietly, "because that's what I should have done."

Wow! If Mr. Ott had ducked from that pitch that hit him in the head, his whole life might have turned out differently. It was sad.

"Some kids at Dirk School challenged our class to a softball game," said Michael. "Will you coach us?"

Mr. Ott wiped his face with a handkerchief. He took a long time before answering.

"I'm an old man now," he said. "I'm tired. My days on the ball field are long gone. Besides, my wife, Wilma, would never let me."

I guess that was that. Mr. Ott wasn't going to coach us. We started making our way back down the steps.

"Pssssst!" Andrea whispered to me. "Do a puppy dog face."

Of course! I looked at Mr. Ott and put

on my best puppy dog face. We all put on puppy dog faces.

"Please, please, *please*?" we begged.

"Well . . . *okay*," said Mr. Ott. "I'll coach you. Just don't tell Wilma. And stop making those puppy dog faces."

"YAY!" we all shouted, which is also "YAY" backward.

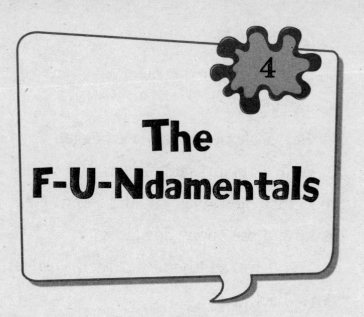

The F-U-Ndamentals

Mr. Ott said to meet him in our playground after school. When the dismissal bell rang, he was out there waiting for us. He had a bunch of bats, balls, gloves, and batting helmets. We sat around him on the grass.

"How many of you youngsters have played ball before?" Mr. Ott asked.

I've played Pee Wee football, but hardly any softball. Only Andrea raised her hand. She smiled the smile she smiles to let everybody know she did something nobody else did.

"That's okay," said Mr. Ott. "I'll whip you kids into shape."

"Is that legal?" I asked.

"It's just an expression, Arlo!" said Andrea.

"Baseball is all about the number three," Mr. Ott explained. "You got three strikes and three outs. You got nine players and nine innings. Three times three is nine."

Man, this was sounding like a math lesson.

"There's ninety feet between the bases,"

continued Mr. Ott. "That's thirty times three. *Blah blah blah blah blah blah...*"

He went on like that for a million hundred minutes. I thought I was gonna die from old age. We had less than a week to get ready for our game. When were we gonna learn how to hit, throw, and catch?

"Can we play ball already?" asked Michael.

"First, you need to learn the fundamentals," replied Mr. Ott. "Fundamentals starts with F-U-N. Let's start by throwing and catching."

Finally!

He picked up a laundry bag from the grass. And you'll never believe what he pulled out of the bag.

It was a turtle!

"Ooooh, I love turtles!" said Andrea.

"Good," said Mr. Ott. "Think fast!"

He threw the turtle up in the air. Andrea freaked out for a moment, and then she caught the turtle just before it hit the ground.*

"Good job!" said Mr. Ott. "You caught the turtle with both hands."

"Uh, shouldn't we play catch with a *ball*?" asked Michael.

"No!" barked Mr. Ott. "If you drop a ball, it doesn't matter. But nobody wants to drop a turtle."

I guess that made sense, in a weird way. Turtles are cool. One time, we did turtle

---

*Don't try this at home! Leave your turtles alone!

yoga at school. We had turtles climbing on our backs. (You can read about it in a book called *Ms. Jo-Jo Is a Yo-Yo!*)

Mr. Ott told us to pair up so we could toss turtles back and forth. My turtle tossing partner was Neil.

"Don't let your turtle hit the ground!"

Mr. Ott shouted as he watched us toss the turtles. "If you can catch a turtle, you can catch a ball."

Andrea was the best turtle tosser, of course. But we were all pretty good, because nobody wanted their turtle to hit the ground and get hurt.

Mr. Ott said it was time for us to work on hitting.

"Everybody grab a bat," he said.

We all picked up bats.

"Okay, put the knob end of the bat on your toe," said Mr. Ott, "and see if you can balance the bat on your foot."

What?

I tried to balance the bat on my foot. It

was hard! The bat kept falling off.

"What does this have to do with hitting a ball?" asked Alexia.

"You need to have good balance to be a good hitter," said Mr. Ott.

We balanced bats on our feet for a million hundred minutes. After a while, I got the hang of it. Andrea was the best bat balancer, of course. She could even balance a bat on her nose.

"Now you're getting it!" shouted Mr. Ott.

He went to his car and took a

weird-looking machine out of the trunk. He dragged it over to the field.

"What's that?" asked Neil.

"This is Robbie RoboThrow," said Mr. Ott. "He's a mechanical pitcher."

He set up Robbie RoboThrow and loaded it with softballs. Then he turned it on. Robbie made some weird noises. Then a bunch of wheels spun around, and Robbie threw a softball right over the plate. It was cool.

"Who wants to hit first?" asked Mr. Ott.

"Me! Me! Me!" we all shouted.

Well, everybody shouted "Me!" except Emily.

"I'm afraid," she said. "I don't want to

get hit by the ball."

"The ball should be afraid of getting hit by *you*," said Mr. Ott. "There's nothing to be worried about. Robbie only throws strikes. Go ahead. Get into the batter's box, young lady."

Emily picked up a bat and stepped into the batter's box. Mr. Ott turned on Robbie RoboThrow.

"Keep your eye on the ball," he shouted.

"Won't that hurt?" I asked, but nobody laughed.

Robbie threw a ball. Emily swung and missed.

"You were a little late," Mr. Ott said. "Try again. I'll slow it down."

Mr. Ott adjusted something on Robbie RoboThrow. That's when the weirdest thing in the history of the world happened. Robbie threw a pitch.

Well, that's not the weird part. Robbie is *supposed* to throw pitches. But then it threw another one. And another one. And *another* one.

Softballs were flying at Emily one after the other! Some of them went over the plate. Some of them went over Emily's head. Or behind her. Or right *at* her.

"Watch out, Emily!" shouted Andrea.

"Help!" Emily shouted as she dropped the bat and covered her head with her arms.

"Robbie's out of control!" shouted Michael.

"Turn it off!" shouted Ryan.

"Do something, Mr. Ott!" shouted Alexia.

"I'm trying!" shouted Mr. Ott.

Robbie RoboThrow was shooting softballs at Emily, rapid-fire.

Everybody was yelling and screaming and hooting and hollering and freaking out.

Finally, Robbie RoboThrow ran out of

softballs. We all rushed over to Emily. She was crying and she had a bruise on her arm, but it looked like she was going to be okay.

"Rub some dirt on it," said Mr. Ott. "You'll be fine."

"Why do they call it softball?" Emily whimpered as we helped her up. "The ball isn't soft."

A Secret Language

Grown-ups always say practice makes perfect. And you know what? For once, they were right!

We practiced after school with Mr. Ott on Tuesday, Wednesday, and Thursday. And we were getting *good*. We hardly ever dropped our turtles. Mr. Ott taught us how to run the bases and how to bunt. Andrea was the best bunter, of *course*.

"Can you teach us how to spit?" I asked Mr. Ott. "Baseball players spit all the time."

"Maybe tomorrow," said Mr. Ott. "Today, you need to learn how to slide."

Oooh, sliding is *cool*. When there's a close play, you're supposed to slide into the base to make it harder for the fielder to tag you.

"I don't want to get my pants dirty," said Neil.

"Yeah," agreed Emily. "Dirt is dirty."

"That's why they call it *dirt*!" shouted Mr. Ott.

He told us that sliding was dangerous,

so we had to be really careful. He set up a slip 'n slide on the grass. Do you know what a slip 'n slide is? If you don't, what is your problem? Look it up! *Everybody* knows what a slip 'n slide is. It has the perfect name!

Anyway, Mr. Ott showed us how to do a bent-leg slide. That's when you fold one leg under the other knee so your legs make a shape like the number four. Then you slide on your butt and touch the base with your toe.

Sliding is fun, especially when you're sliding on a slip 'n slide. We all lined up and slid over and over again. Even Emily looked like she was enjoying herself.

"Hit the dirt!" Mr. Ott shouted when it was time for us to slide.

After a while, we were getting good at sliding. Andrea was the best slider, of *course*.

"Okay, gather 'round," said Mr. Ott. "Take a knee."

"How can we take a knee?" I asked. "Knees aren't removable."

"It's just an expression, Arlo!" said Andrea.

I knew that. I was just yanking Andrea's chain. We all gathered around Mr. Ott, like a football team in a huddle. He lowered his voice to a whisper.

"Okay, you kids have mastered the fundamentals," he said. "Now it's time for me to teach you some signs."

"Signs?" we all said. Nobody knew what he was talking about.

"It's like a secret language that only we

45

understand," said Mr. Ott. "We don't want the Dirk team to know what we're planning to do."

Secret languages are cool. Our bus driver, Mrs. Kormel, invented her own secret language. (You can read about it in a book called *Mrs. Kormel Is Not Normal!*)

"When I touch my nose," Mr. Ott said as he touched his nose, "it means swing at the next pitch. And if I touch the brim of my cap, it means bunt the next pitch. Got that?"

We all got it.

"If I tug on my left ear," Mr. Ott said as he tugged on his left ear, "it means take."

"Take *what*?" I asked.

"Take the next pitch," he replied.

"Where should we take it?" I asked.

"Taking a pitch means you don't swing at it, Arlo!" Andrea told me, rolling her eyes.

Oh. Why didn't he say so?

"If I put my hands on my hips," Mr. Ott said as he put his hands on his hips, "it means steal a base."

"Stealing is wrong," said Alexia. "That's what my parents tell me."

"Well," said Mr. Ott, "the ball field is the *one* place it's okay for you to steal."

Cool! It's sort of like when your grandma gives you a horrible sweater for your birthday and you're supposed to say you like it.

That's the one time it's okay for you to lie.

"If I fold my arms across my chest," Mr. Ott said as he folded his arms across his chest, "it means go to the snack bar and get me a taco."

"Why do we need a sign for that?" asked Alexia.

"Who's the coach here, you or me?" said Mr. Ott. "Just learn the signs, okay?"

Then Mr. Ott waved his hand back and forth behind his back.

"What does that sign mean?" Neil asked.

"Oh," said Mr. Ott. "That means I just farted."*

----

*Every book is required to have one fart joke. That's the law.

Mr. Ott was going over some more signs when I happened to look over his shoulder. In the distance, in the trees next to the playground, I saw a person. Or the face of a person anyway.

Somebody was watching us! I couldn't even tell if it was a man or a woman. The person was looking through binoculars.

"Hey, look!" I shouted, pointing to the trees.

Nobody was there.

Puppy Dog Faces

Everybody turned around to see who was watching us from the trees.

"Who was that, A.J.?" asked Ryan.

"I don't know," I replied. "All I saw was a face, with binoculars in front of it."

"I bet it was Morgan Brocklebank!" Andrea said. "She was spying on us!"

"Why would she do that?" asked Emily.

"She was trying to steal our signs," said Mr. Ott. "It happens all the time."

"Those Dirk dorks will do *anything* to win," said Michael. "Now I *really* want to beat them."

We were all angry.

We were even *more* angry the next day when Mr. Klutz came into our classroom and told us that Dirk School had raised over two hundred dollars to find a cure for freckles.*

"Wait, tell me again why we're raising money to fight freckles?" asked Alexia.

"There's nothing wrong with having freckles," said Ryan.

---

*That's almost a million.

"That's a dumb charity," said Neil. "I *like* my freckles."

"Me too, but we can't let Dirk win," said Andrea. "We have to raise more money than they do."

Mr. Klutz got permission for us to set up a table outside the Piggly Wiggly supermarket. He also got donations of food from Porky's Pork Sausages and Jiggly Gelatin so we could sell their products and raise money.

The whole team went to Piggly Wiggly after practice. Lots of customers were going in and out with their shopping carts.

"Okay, let's work on our puppy dog

faces," said Andrea.

"Why?" asked Emily.

"Because if anybody says they don't want to buy food from us, we can put on our puppy dog faces."

Andrea was right about that. Grown-ups can't resist a puppy dog face.

A lady came out of the Piggly Wiggly pushing her shopping cart. We jumped in front of her.

"We're raising money to fight freckles," Alexia said. "Would you like to buy some Jiggly Gelatin?"

"I'm sorry," the lady replied. "I don't like Jiggly Gelatin."

"But it's for *charity*!" Ryan told her.

"No, thank you."

"It's only a dollar," said Emily.

We all put on our best puppy dog faces.

"Please, please, please?"

"Okay," the lady said. "I'll take a box."

"Yay!"

"Thank you!" Alexia said when the lady took a dollar out of her purse.

A man came out of the Piggly Wiggly carrying two shopping bags.

"We're raising money to fight freckles," Neil said to him. "Will you buy some Porky's Pork Sausages?"

"I'm allergic to pork," the man said as he walked by.

"But it's for *charity*!" Ryan told him.

"No, thanks."

"It's just two dollars," said Emily.

We all put on puppy dog faces.

"Please, please, please?"

"Oh, all right," the man said as he took
the bills out of his wallet. "Gimme one."

"Yay!"

A husband and wife came out of the Piggly Wiggly. They were pushing a shopping cart with a baby sitting in the front.

"We're selling Porky's Pork Sausages and Jiggly Gelatin," Andrea said. "Will you buy some?"

"We're in a hurry," the lady told us. "It's nap time."

"May I show you a short video?" Andrea asked.

Andrea took out her smartphone and held it up for the husband and wife to see. It was a video that Dirk School had made. The voice of Morgan Brocklebank played over sad music and a film of a little girl with tears running down her face.

"Do you know anyone who has . . . freckles?" said Morgan Brocklebank. "Every night, little Suzie goes to bed with freckles. Millions of people suffer from freckles every day. They have no hope. But it doesn't have to be that way. With your help, we can fund research and wipe out freckles in our lifetime. Just pennies will make a difference for little Suzie, and other kids like her all over the world."

"I'm not giving money for freckle research," the husband said.

We put on our best puppy dog faces and said, "Please, please, please?" The wife looked at her husband. She was making a puppy dog face too.

"Honey, it's for *charity*," she told him.

"Okay, okay!" he groaned. "How much?"

"Just one dollar for a box of Jiggly Gelatin," I told him.

He pulled a dollar out of his wallet and gave it to us.

"Yay!"

We sold *tons* of Porky's Pork Sausages and Jiggly Gelatin. Nobody could say no when they saw our puppy dog faces.

After an hour, we counted up the money. We had raised two hundred and sixty-eight dollars.

That's almost a million!

Game Day

It was Saturday, the day of the big game.

After breakfast (best meal of the day), my parents drove me to Dirk School. When we got there, each of us had to pay a dollar to get into the playground.

"What?!" I said. "We have to *pay*?"

"It's for charity," my mother told me as

she took three dollars out of her purse. She put the bills in a big red box that said Freckle Fund on it.

"Thank you!" said the smiley Dirk mom at the table. "We've raised over a thousand dollars!"

The bleachers were filled with parents and friends.* A bunch of our teachers were there too. Some people were holding signs.

DIRK SCHOOL RULES!
I LOVE YOU, MORGAN!
DOWN WITH FRECKLES!

---

*Why are they called bleachers? They must clean them with bleach. That makes no sense at all.

"Get your hot cross buns here!" shouted Ryan's mom, Mrs. Dole. She was walking around the stands selling homemade baked goods. (You can read about her in a book called *Mrs. Dole Is Out of Control!*)

My parents wished me good luck, and I ran off to join our team on the bench. Everybody was gathered around Mr. Ott.

"Are you kids ready?" he asked.

"Yeah!" we shouted back.

"I CAN'T *HEAR* YOU!" shouted Mr. Ott. "I SAID ARE YOU KIDS *READY*?"

"YEAH!" we shouted, even louder.

Grown-ups are always saying they can't hear us. I guess when you get old, you start to lose your hearing.

The Dirk School band was sitting in the bleachers, and they played that song "We Are the Champions." A door at the back of the school opened, and the Dirk team marched out. They were wearing matching uniforms and chanting.

Let's get dirty!
Let's get mean!
Come on, Dirk!
Let's beat this team!

"Oh no," groaned Emily. "Can't we quit right now? The score is zero to zero. We can say it was a tie."

"Don't be silly," said Mr. Ott. "Those kids

put on their pants one leg at a time, just like you."

Huh? What does that have to do with anything?

As the Dirk team marched past the front of the bleachers, Morgan Brocklebank handed out baseball cards with her own picture on them.

We're rough!
We're tough!
Come on, Dirk!
Let's strut our stuff!

"A.J. and Andrea," said Mr. Ott, "let's go out there and shake hands."

"I don't want to shake hands," I said.

"Do we have to?" asked Andrea.

"It's called sportsmanship," Mr. Ott told us. "Follow me!"

The three of us walked out to the pitcher's mound. The Dirk coach came over with Morgan and this kid named Tommy, who always has a finger in his nose.

"Welcome to our cemetery," sneered Morgan.

"Why do you call it a cemetery?" asked Andrea.

"Because we're gonna *bury* you here," replied Morgan.

"No trash talking, kids," said Mr. Ott. "Everybody shake hands."

I *really* didn't want to shake hands with Tommy the Nosepicker. So I went to shake Morgan's hand.

"You losers are going *down!*" she said, looking me in the eye as she squeezed my hand really hard. I thought I was gonna die. I squeezed back as hard as I could.

"That's what *you* think," I said, pretending my hand didn't hurt.

We were about to go back to our bench when Morgan stopped and turned around.

"Hey, A.J.," she said. "Would you care to make it . . . *interesting?*"

"I already think it's interesting," I told her.

"That means she wants to make a bet on the game," Andrea told me.

Oh. I knew that.

"How about the losing team has to clean a toilet bowl at the other school," suggested Morgan, "with a toothbrush."

I looked at Andrea. Andrea looked at me. Andrea and I looked at Mr. Ott. Mr. Ott looked at me and Andrea. We were all looking at each other.

"So, what do you say?" asked Morgan. "Do we have a deal?"

"Deal!" I said.

Andrea and I walked back to our bench. I rubbed my hand, trying to get the circulation back in my fingers.

Mr. Ott led us in some stretching exercises. He said it's really important to stretch before you play any game. While we were stretching, Morgan came off the Dirk bench. She was holding one of those cannons that shoots T-shirts into the crowd.

"Who wants a T-shirt?" she hollered.

"Me! Me! Me!" everybody shouted.

Morgan shot a T-shirt high into the bleachers. Then she loaded up another T-shirt, wheeled around, and pointed the cannon at us.

"You asked for it!" she shouted.

A T-shirt came shooting out of the cannon.

"Watch out!" Ryan shouted.

"Run for your lives!" hollered Neil.

We all dove out of the way. The T-shirt bounced off Emily's head.

"I'm hit!" she shouted as she fell down.

We all gathered around Emily.

"Emily is hurt!" Andrea shouted. "We have to forfeit the game."

"No way!" said Mr. Ott. "Do you know what they call people who quit?"

"Quitters?" I asked.

"That's right!" said Mr. Ott. He leaned over Emily and asked, "Emily, what day is it?"

"Uh . . ." said Emily. "Saturday?"

"She'll be fine," said Mr. Ott, helping her off the ground. "Rub some dirt on it. That's taking one for the team, Emily."

Emily was shaken up. But at least she got a free T-shirt.

Mr. Ott told us to warm up by throwing a ball back and forth. I went to play catch with Ryan. That's when the weirdest thing in the history of the world happened.

A long limousine pulled up next to the field. I didn't know any celebrities were coming to the game. We all wondered who it was. And you'll never believe in a million hundred years who got out of the limo.

It was Mayor Hubble!

He's the mayor of our town. He's always cutting ribbons, posing for pictures, getting arrested, and doing other mayor stuff. (You can read about him in a book called *Mayor Hubble Is in Trouble!*)

"I thought Mayor Hubble was in jail," I said to Ryan.

"He got time off for good behavior," Ryan told me.

Mayor Hubble was dressed in black, and he was holding a catcher's mask. He walked over to home plate and dusted it off with a brush.

"What's he doing?" I asked Mr. Ott.

"He's the umpire."

Oh! Mayor Hubble shook hands with a bunch of Dirk parents and posed for pictures next to the Freckle Fund box.

"How much money did these kids raise?" he asked.

"Altogether," said one of the

Dirk parents, "they raised almost two thousand dollars!"

"WOW!" everybody said, which is "MOM" upside down.

"That's *impressive*!" said Mayor Hubble.

Our team lined up on the first-base line. The Dirk dorks lined up on the third-base line. We took off our caps while the Dirk band played "The Star-Spangled Banner."

". . . the la-hand of the free . . . and the home . . . of the . . . brave!"

Mayor Hubble put on his mask and shouted, "Play ball!"

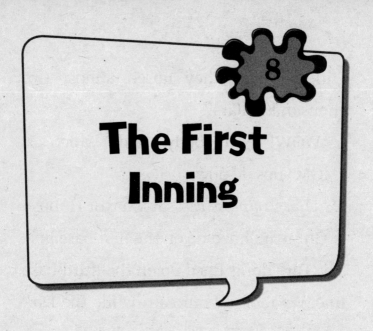

The First Inning

Even though Dirk was the home team, they said we could bat first or take the field first. Mr. Ott said we should take the field first. He gathered us around him.

"Okay, kids," he said. "We came to play. Stay focused. Get it done. You know how to win. Stay in the moment. Play your game. Take care of business. Give it a hundred and ten percent. There's no tomorrow."

Boy, he sure knows a lot of sports clichés.

"Who's on first?" I asked Ryan.

"I don't know," he replied.

Andrea was our best turtle tosser, so Mr. Ott said she would be our pitcher. He told Emily to be the catcher. He told me to play first base, Ryan to play second, and Michael to play third. Alexia was our shortstop.* Neil went out to center field. There was nobody to play left field

---

*Why does it take longer to run from second to third base than it takes to run from first to second? Because there's a short stop in the middle!

or right field, so Mayor Hubble said two grown-ups could play for each team. Mr. Cooper and Mr. Klutz ran out to the outfield. Andrea threw a couple of warm-up pitches.

Morgan Brocklebank was the lead-off batter for Dirk. She looked mean, and she looked like she knew how to hit.

"Strike her out, Andrea!" Neil shouted.

"No batter. No batter!" hollered Alexia.

"We want a pitcher," somebody yelled from the Dirk bench, "not a glass of water!"

Andrea threw hard, but Morgan Brocklebank smashed the first pitch into the outfield. Neil chased it down, but by the time he got to the ball, Morgan was standing on third base. A triple!

Tommy the Nosepicker was up next. He took his finger out of his nose long enough to hit a single. Morgan Brocklebank scored easily from third. Dirk was leading 1–0.

Andrea struck out the next three Dirk kids, and it was our turn to bat. We all put on batting helmets. The Dirk pitcher was Morgan, of course. The Dirk dorks started chanting again.

We know karate!
We know kung fu!
But we're playing softball,
And we're gonna mess with you!

"Hey, our team needs a chant," said Alexia.

"Yeah," everybody agreed.

"You're good at writing poems, Arlo," said Andrea. "Why don't you make up a chant?"

Well, she was right about that. I make up cool raps all the time. That's how I got into the gifted and talented program. I stood up and started rapping.

Cotton candy!

Cracker jacks!

Hey there, pitcher!

Yack, yack, yack!

Oh, boy, Morgan sure looks mean!

Her arm is like a washing machine!

I thought everybody was going to stand up and chant with me. But nobody stood up. Nobody chanted. Everybody was looking at me. I hate when that happens. I sat back down.

"That chant was lame, dude," Ryan told me.

There was no time to come up with a better chant. Alexia, our lead-off batter, stepped up to the plate.

"You're in the driver's seat, Alexia!" hollered Mr. Ott.

Huh? That made no sense at all. We're too young to drive.

Morgan went into her windup, and Alexia swung at the first pitch. She hit a grounder to second. It looked like an easy play, but the second baseman bobbled the ball and Alexia was safe. We all cheered.

Ryan was up next. When he stepped into the batter's box, I noticed that Mr. Ott had his hands on his hips—the steal sign!

On the first pitch to Ryan, Alexia took off from first base. The Dirk catcher tried to throw her out, but Alexia slid in safely. I looked over at Mr. Ott. He was touching the brim of his hat—the bunt sign!

Ryan tried to bunt three times, but he struck out. Bunting is *hard*. Michael was up next. He watched a couple of pitches go by without swinging. It was one ball and one strike.

I looked over at Mr. Ott. He folded his arms across his chest. The taco sign! Neil ran over to the snack bar and got a taco for Mr. Ott.

Morgan wound up for her next pitch.

Michael took a swing at it and hit the ball right over first base.

"Go! Go! Go!" we all screamed.

Alexia rounded third base and slid into home. The throw was late.

"Safe!" shouted Mayor Hubble.

The game was tied at 1–1.

A Seesaw Battle

I won't bore you with all the details, but it was an exciting game! Dirk scored two runs in the second inning to take the lead. And then we came back and tied it up again. Then they scored another run.

Then we were leading again.

Then they tied it up.

Then we were leading again.

Then they tied it up.

Then we were leading again.

Then they tied it up.

Then we were leading again.

Then they tied it up.

Aren't you tired of reading this?

Then we were leading again.

Then they were leading again.

Then we were leading again.

Then they were leading again.

I know I am.

Then we were leading again.

Then they were leading again.

Then we were leading again.

Then they were leading again.

It's got to end at some point.

Then we were leading again.

Then they were leading again.

Then we were leading again.

Then they tied it up.

"This is quite a seesaw battle," said Mr. Ott.

What? We weren't fighting on seesaws. That would be weird.

Mr. Ott is a crackpot.*

---

*Aren't you glad this chapter is over?

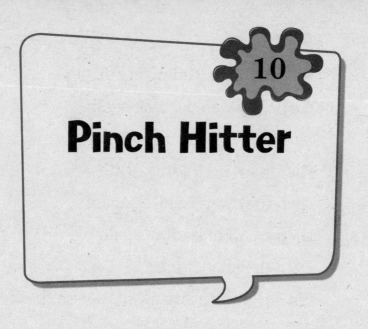

Pinch Hitter

It was the last inning. The score was tied.

"Okay, we get last licks," Neil shouted as we ran off the field.

"Gross!" I said. "I don't want to lick anything."

"That means we get the last turn at bat, dumbhead," Andrea told me.

I was going to say something mean to Andrea, but Mr. Ott gathered the team around him so he could say more sports clichés.

"Okay, kids," Mr. Ott said. "Wait for your pitch. Put the bat on the ball. Make contact. Take it one run at a time. This is for all the marbles."

Huh? Marbles? I had no idea what he was talking about. Ryan stepped up to the plate.

"Ryan! Ryan! Ryan!" we chanted.

"You can do it, Ryan!" Neil shouted.

But Ryan couldn't do it. He grounded out to shortstop. One out. The Dirk dorks started chanting again.

You might be good at soccer!
You might be good at track!
But when it comes to softball,
You better watch your back!

Michael stepped up to the plate.

"Michael! Michael! Michael!"

Michael struck out. Now there were two outs. It was Andrea's turn at bat.

"Andrea! Andrea! Andrea!"

"Get a hit, Andrea!" shouted Emily.

"It ain't over till it's over!" shouted Mr. Ott.

That's when the weirdest thing in the history of the world happened. A lady climbed over the fence and ran onto the field.

"Oh no," groaned Mr. Ott.

"Who's that?" I asked him. "Some obsessed fan?"

"No," he replied. "It's my wife, Wilma."

WHAT?!

Mrs. Ott ran all the way across the field until she reached our bench.

"Willie Ott!" she screamed.

"How did you know I was here, Wilma?" he asked.

"I was watching you with binoculars all week," said Mrs. Ott. "I thought you were running around carousing."

I didn't know what carousing meant, but it sounded pretty bad.

"No," he told Wilma. "I've been running around with these kids."

"Willie Ott, you go sit down on that bench!" she ordered.

Mr. Ott sat on the bench.

"From now on, *I'm* coaching this team," said Mrs. Ott. "Get up there, girl, and get a hit!"

Andrea stepped up to the plate. Morgan

Brocklebank went into her windup and let the pitch fly. Andrea swung.

And she connected!

The ball took off like a bullet down the third-base line! The third baseman dove, but the ball skipped past him. Andrea raced for first. By the time the Dirk players got to the ball, she was standing on second base. We were yelling and screaming our heads off.

"Okay, who's up?" asked Mrs. Ott.

"I am," said Mr. Cooper, getting off the bench.

"Not anymore," said Mrs. Ott. "Sit down."

Mr. Cooper sat down.

Mayor Hubble walked over to our bench.

"What's the problem?" he asked.

"There's no problem," said Mrs. Ott. "I'm bringing in a pinch hitter."

"Who?" asked Mayor Hubble.

"My husband," she replied. "Willie Ott."

WHAT?!

Mrs. Ott picked up a bat and handed it to Mr. Ott.

"Get up there and hit," she ordered.

"B-b-but—but, Wilma . . ."

We all giggled because Mr. Ott said "but," which sounds just like "butt" even though there's only one *T*.

"I can't hit," Mr. Ott said. "I'm an old man."

Wilma put her hand on Mr. Ott's shoulder.

"Willie," she said. "You never forgave yourself for what happened in that World Series game so many years ago. This is your chance to make up for it. You're *never* too old. Your whole life has been leading to this moment."

Mr. Ott sighed.

"If you say so, dear," he said, taking the bat.

So there we were. It was the bottom of the ninth.

Score tied.

Two outs.

It was all up to Mr. Ott.

"Ott! Ott! Ott!" we chanted.

"Drive me in, Mr. Ott!" Andrea shouted

from second base.

On the pitcher's mound, Morgan Brocklebank looked mad. I thought she might try to hit Mr. Ott in the head.

"He's a choker!" a Dirk parent shouted. "He choked in the World Series, and he'll choke now. Duck! Duck! Duck!"

The Dirk parents started chanting "Duck!" That was mean. Mr. Ott looked angry as he stepped into the batter's box.

"Just ignore them, sweetie," shouted Mrs. Ott. "You can do it!"

"Sweetie! Sweetie! Sweetie!" the Dirk kids chanted.

Morgan Brocklebank went into her windup and threw her first pitch. Mr. Ott didn't duck. He just watched the ball go by. Mayor Hubble called strike one.

Morgan went into her windup and threw her second pitch. Mr. Ott watched it go by. Mayor Hubble called ball one.

DUCK! DUCK! DUCK!

Morgan threw her third pitch. Mr. Ott watched it go by. Mayor Hubble called ball two.

It didn't look like Mr. Ott wanted to swing.

Morgan threw another pitch. Mr. Ott watched it go by.

"Strike two!" shouted Mayor Hubble. "The count is two balls and two strikes."

Morgan threw again and Mr. Ott watched it go by. Ball three.

"You can't hit the ball with the bat on your shoulder, Willie!" shouted Mrs. Ott.

Full count. This was it. There was electricity in the air.

Well, not really. If there was electricity

in the air, we would have been electro-cuted. But everybody was glued to their seats.

Well, not exactly. Why would people glue themselves to seats? How would you get the glue off your pants? But it was intense.*

Morgan went into her windup.

Mr. Ott tightened his grip on the bat.

Morgan threw.

Mr. Ott swung.

AND HE HIT THE BALL!

It was a hard grounder down the first-base line. The Dirk first baseman went

---

*Which is not the same thing as being in tents. Why would they have tents on a ball field?

over to grab it. But he didn't get his glove down fast enough. The ball got past him!

"Go! Go! Go!" we screamed.

Andrea took off from second base.

The Dirk right fielder picked up the ball.

Andrea was rounding third base.

The right fielder threw the ball home.

"Go, Andrea! Go!" we all screamed.

Andrea was about ten feet from home plate. So was the ball. It was going to be close.

"Slide, Andrea! Slide!"

Andrea slid home, kicking up a cloud of dust. The Dirk catcher caught the ball on one hop and tagged Andrea on her leg at the same time her foot touched home plate.

It was the most exciting moment in the history of the world!

"Safe!" we screamed.

"Out!" the Dirk kids screamed.

Of course, it was up to Mayor Hubble to decide if Andrea was safe or out.

"Hey!" somebody shouted. "Where's the umpire?"

Mayor Hubble was *gone*!

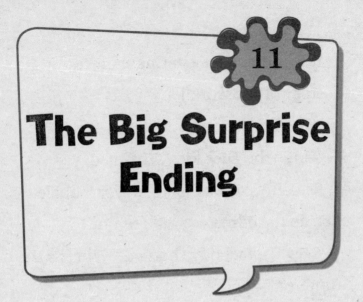

The Big Surprise Ending

We looked around for Mayor Hubble. Nobody knew if Andrea was safe or out, because there was no umpire behind home plate.

"Where's Mayor Hubble?" everybody was asking. "Where did he go?"

We were all yelling and screaming and

hooting and hollering and freaking out.

"Maybe he went to the bathroom," I suggested.

But Mayor Hubble wasn't in the bathroom. He wasn't in the bleachers either. And he wasn't at the snack bar.

"Look!" Morgan Brocklebank shouted.

She was pointing toward the parking lot. We all looked. Mayor Hubble was getting into his limousine. And he had the Freckle Fund box under his arm!

"Mayor Hubble is stealing our money!" shouted Morgan.

"Get him!" everyone shouted.

A bunch of kids and parents from both schools ran to the parking lot and chased

Mayor Hubble's limo. The wheels kicked up dirt and gravel as the limo peeled away. I saw it with my own eyes!

Well, it would be pretty hard to see it with somebody else's eyes.

I didn't bother chasing after Mayor Hubble. Neither did Andrea. What's the use?

Mayor Hubble always steals stuff, and he always seems to get away with it.

Andrea and I sat down on the bench.

"Well, it was a good game anyway," I said.

"Hey, look!" Andrea said, pointing to first base.

I looked. And you'll never believe who was standing out there. It was Mr. Ott and Mrs. Ott! And you'll never believe what they were doing.

They were kissing!*

"Isn't that romantic, Arlo?" asked Andrea.

---

*Ugh, gross.

Well, that's pretty much what happened. We didn't win the game, but we didn't lose it either. At least we won't have to clean a toilet bowl at Dirk School with a toothbrush. The best part was that Mr. Ott got a big hit with the pressure on. He looked really happy.

Maybe Mayor Hubble will get caught and wind up in jail again. Maybe we'll get through page twenty-three in our math books. Maybe Mr. Ott will teach us how to spit. Maybe Mr. Klutz will stop walking into doors. Maybe grown-ups will get their ears checked and stop saying they can't hear us all the time. Maybe we can eat brunch, linner, lupper, lunner, brinner, lunfast, dunch, or dinch. Maybe they'll find a cure for freckles.

But it won't be easy!